MOLLY IN THE MIDDLE

MOLLY IN THE MIDDLE

WRITTEN AND ILLUSTRATED
BY
ELEANOR FRANCES LATTIMORE

WILLIAM MORROW AND COMPANY
New York: 1956

Seventh Printing, August 1967

Published simultaneously in the Dominion of Canada
by George J. McLeod Limited, Toronto.

Printed in the United States of America.

Library of Congress Catalog Card Number: 56-6739

CHAPTERS

By the Same Author

WILLOW TREE VILLAGE
DIANA IN THE CHINA SHOP
HOLLY IN THE SNOW
JASPER
WU, THE GATEKEEPER'S SON
LIVELY VICTORIA
BELLS FOR A CHINESE DONKEY
THE FIG TREE
CHRISTOPHER AND HIS TURTLE
INDIGO HILL
DEBORAH'S WHITE WINTER
DAVY OF THE EVERGLADES
THREE LITTLE CHINESE GIRLS
JEREMY'S ISLE
BAYOU BOY

1

NINE BROTHERS AND SISTERS

Molly Hubbard opened her diary, which her mother had given her on her last birthday. It was a small book with a red leather binding and all its pages were perfectly blank. Molly had been too busy going to school to have time for keeping a diary. Now it was June, though, and the holidays had begun, so Molly planned to write in her diary every single day.

She licked her pencil and wrote *My Diary* in capital letters. She was up in the big apple tree behind her house and it was a quiet, private place for writing. The tree was old, with a twisted, knotted trunk, but its leaves were as green and clustering as when it was young, and they almost hid Molly. She hoped no one would notice the ladder leaning against the tree and guess where she was.

Molly was not an ordinary little girl. She was the middle one in a family of nine children, which made her different from any of her friends. Carol was an only child, Sarah had one brother, but Molly had a sister and seven brothers! It was no wonder that she liked privacy now and then, even though she enjoyed being in a large family.

The Hubbards lived in a big old-fashioned house in a small New Hampshire town. It was the right kind of house for a large family to live in, because it had fourteen rooms, not counting the attic. There was a front porch as well as a back porch, and there was a widow's walk on the roof. Molly liked to go up on the widow's walk. She could not see the river from there, but she could see the hills beyond the roof tops of the town.

Her father called Molly a little brown wren, because she was small and quick, with brown hair and brown eyes. Since it was summer, she wore her hair in pigtails for coolness, but it curled in little ringlets around her forehead. Molly did not like her curly hair at all. She wished her hair were smooth and golden, like Alicia's. Alicia was her sister. She was two years older than Molly, and Molly admired her very much.

Alicia and Molly had three big brothers and four little brothers. The three big boys were named Tom, Rufus, and Reginald. They did not have time to pay much attention to their sisters, for they were always riding off on their bicycles to play ball or to go swimming with their friends. But they always came home promptly at mealtime.

Edward was the oldest of the four little ones. He would have preferred to tag along with Tom and Rufus and Reginald, but since they kept leaving him behind, he played with the twins. The twins, Gordon and Gregory, came directly after Edward. Their favorite game was Cowboys and Indians, and their favorite place was an Indian tent in the back yard.

Molly peeked cautiously from her tree. She could see the tent, but she did not see any sign of Edward or the twins. A hush lay over the back yard and Molly was glad of that, for she thought that if the twins and Edward spied the ladder they would climb right up and bother her. Even John might want to climb the ladder, Molly thought.

John was the baby. He had just learned how to walk, and he kept on walking as though he would never stop. Somebody had to keep an eye on him every minute to see that he did not fall downstairs or trot into the street. His brothers and sisters all took turns in minding John, though he was Alicia's special charge.

Molly wrote in her diary: "I, Molly Hubbard, am a little girl with one sister and seven brothers. We have fun." She stopped and wondered what to write next. She had planned to write about everything that happened during the summer, but there had not been time for anything to happen yet.

Her best friend, Carol, had gone away to camp and her second-best friend, Sarah, was going to the mountains. What a lot they would have to write about if they kept diaries! Molly closed her diary and slipped it into her pocket. She wished that something would happen.

Just then a war whoop sounded below the tree. "I see you, Molly!" cried a voice, as a toy arrow hit the trunk and fell to the ground.

Molly peered down through the leaves and saw a small boy in an Indian suit, with a feather headdress. It was Edward, who had discovered her hiding place.

"I didn't hear you coming," said Molly.

"That's because I'm an Indian," said Edward. "I crept toward the tree, and you couldn't hear me creeping."

"Yip-ee!" Here came the twins, with cowboy hats and pistols. It was hard to tell which

one was Gordon and which was Gregory. "Don't climb up here," Molly told them. "I'm coming down."

"Oh, no, you're not," said Edward, with a big smile. He pushed the ladder and it fell over with a crash.

"Look out for the twins!" Molly cried. But the twins had darted out of the way in the nick of time.

"Put that ladder right back," said Molly sternly.

The twins ran off, snapping their pistols, but Edward stayed behind. "I was just joking. Can't you get down, Molly?" he asked.

"No, I can't," said Molly. "Please put the ladder back."

"What will you give me if I do?"

"Nothing," said Molly.

Edward hesitated, but when he finally spoke, his voice was cheerful. "All right," he said. "I will put the ladder up again and rescue you, Molly."

Although it had been easy for Edward to

push the ladder over, it was very hard for him to lift it by himself. He tugged and strained, but he could not get it up off the ground. "Come back, Twins, and help me!" he called. But the twins did not come back. "Wait here, Molly," said Edward. And then he, too, ran away.

Molly waited. There was nothing else for her to do. Without the ladder, she was stranded in the apple tree. She did not dare to jump, for the ground was too far away, and she did not feel like sliding down the rough, gnarled trunk.

She sat perched in the tree just like the wren her father called her, wishing that she had wings and could fly to the ground. "Edward!" she called, but he did not answer. Molly suddenly realized that Edward and the twins must have forgotten her. If only Alicia would come, she thought. Alicia would rescue her. So Molly called, "Alicia! I am up in the apple tree!"

Still nobody came. The back yard was as

quiet as could be until the dinner bell pealed out, calling the children home.

"Help!" called Molly, above the sound of the ringing bell, and just then other bells rang. They were bicycle bells. The three big boys rode into the yard and jumped off their bicycles —black-haired Tom, red-haired Rufus, and brown-haired Reginald.

They heard Molly's cry for help and they came to her rescue at once, for they could be extremely helpful when they wanted to be. Up went the ladder against the tree, and down the ladder climbed Molly. "Thank you," she said gratefully, when her feet touched the ground.

Molly was glad she had three big brothers. But where were her little brothers? As she had guessed, Edward and the twins had forgotten her. They were playing Cowboys and Indians on the front porch, and only the ringing dinner bell made them stop their game.

2

A FAMILY PICNIC

Each of the older Hubbard children was put in charge of a younger one, and Edward was Molly's special charge. He was a responsibility, because he liked to dawdle and because he was often absent-minded. You never could tell what Edward was going to do next. He seemed to be everywhere, and he seemed to be nowhere. Molly wished that she did not have to keep an eye on Edward. She wished that especially on the day of the picnic.

That was the first Sunday in June. Mother had said at the breakfast table that it would be nice to have a picnic that day. Father agreed, and so did all the children. A picnic was a lot more fun than eating at home.

"Do we have to go to Sunday school first?" asked Edward.

"Yes, you must all go to Sunday school first," said Mother. "While you are there I shall be getting the lunch ready."

"You must stay near me when we have the picnic," Molly warned Edward. "And don't forget about the twins." For Edward was supposed to look after the twins, with a little help from the others.

"It isn't fair for me to have to look after two," Edward complained.

"They are just as easy as one, because they stay together," said Molly.

None of the children dawdled this Sunday morning. They were eager to start on the picnic, and Sunday school came first. Tom, who could take care of himself, saw that Rufus had a clean shirt, and Rufus made sure that Reginald's tie was straight. Even Edward did not lag, though he washed one twin's face twice and never discovered his mistake till they were in Sunday school, where he polished the other twin's face with his handkerchief.

Miss Green, who taught the class, smiled. She was very fond of Edward, whose hair was so fair it was almost silver and who had large blue eyes. He looked like an angel sitting there between his smaller brothers. The twins wiggled and fidgeted, but Edward sat quite still. Edward is never any trouble, thought Miss Green.

When the children returned from Sunday school they found Father in front of the house, stowing picnic baskets in the back of the car. Mother was coming down the steps with John under one arm and a blanket draped over the other. "Change to your old clothes, children," she said. "Everything is ready."

"May Becky come?" asked Alicia. Becky was her best friend, who lived next door.

"Yes, Becky may come if there is room in the car," said Mother.

Although the Sunday picnic was Mother's idea, Father was the one who decided where to have it. "I know where there is a cool, shady place beside a brook," he said. By this time they were all in the car, heading out toward the country. Room had been made for Becky between Alicia and Edward.

Edward felt sad, because his dog Hugo had been left behind. He would rather have had Hugo beside him than Becky. "I don't see why there is room for a girl and not for a dog," he said.

"That's not polite, Edward," said Alicia. "Becky is our guest."

The road climbed up one hill and dipped down another. There were houses on the hilltops and cows on the slopes, but Molly was watching for a brook and she heard the sound of running water before the others did. She saw water falling over a ledge of rock and splashing into a brook that flowed through the valley. While the twins were counting cows, she said, "Look, Father! Is that the brook you meant?"

Father nodded. "Yes, that is the place for our picnic," he said. He parked the car a little way off the highway, and the three big boys carried the baskets to the edge of the brook.

"This is a perfect place for a picnic," said Mother, as she spread out the blanket under a tree. "I wonder why we never came here before."

"I've been here before," said Alicia.

"So have I," said Molly.

"I remember the waterfall," said Edward.

Miss Green lived out in the country and she had invited her class to a picnic near her house the summer before. Molly looked up at a neat white house on the hill above the waterfall. "That is Miss Green's house," she said.

"So it is," said Mother. "But she hasn't come back from town yet. I don't see her car."

"Are we going to eat now?" asked Rufus.

"In about an hour," said Mother.

"May we go in wading?" asked Edward.

"Yes. Take care of the twins."

The children took off their shoes and socks and waded into the brook, while Mother unpacked the picnic lunch. The three big boys started upstream toward the waterfall. "Wait for me!" called Edward. But his brothers did not wait.

"Stay with the twins and me, Edward," said Molly. "Let's play a game, just the four of us." She saw that Alicia and Becky were playing with John, so she thought she ought to keep an eye on the twins as well as Edward. She looked more like a hen than a little brown wren when the little boys gathered around her, and she felt as busy as a hen with three lively chicks.

There were pebbles on the bottom of the brook, and there were smooth, round boulders that made steppingstones from one bank to the other. The game Molly thought of was jumping from boulder to boulder. If you missed or slipped, it did not matter, because the water was shallow and you only got your feet wet.

Molly began to jump from steppingstone to steppingstone, and the twins followed her lead, squealing with excitement. Edward turned to gaze after the three big boys. They were far off, so Edward followed Molly's lead too. He jumped from stone to stone without getting wet, and then he decided to go wading by himself.

Sometimes a thunderstorm comes up quickly in the summer, and that is what happened this particular Sunday. Molly was just about to suggest a new game when she heard the rumble of thunder. A huge, dark cloud was moving over the valley, casting a shadow as dark as itself. As the thunder rumbled again, Molly heard Mother calling, "Come back, children!"

"I'm coming!" Molly answered, but at first she could not move. She was not afraid of the thunder, but the twins were terrified. One of them flung his arms around her from behind, and the other one hugged her knees. As lightning zigzagged toward the earth, they shut their eyes and shivered. "Don't knock me down. There is nothing to be scared of," said Molly. She untangled the twins and seized each one firmly by the hand.

Raindrops had begun to fall, and Molly saw that Mother had picked up John and was wrapping him in the blanket. Alicia and Becky were helping Father pack up the picnic baskets. The lunch had not been eaten yet, and now the day was spoiled. "Hurry up, children! We have got to run," called Mother.

Molly hurried as well as she could with the twins clinging to her. "Come on, Edward," she said, without looking back. "Here are the twins, Mother. Where are we going?"

Father answered her. "Back to the car."

"Where are the boys?" asked Mother.

"Here they are," said Alicia, as Tom and Rufus and Reginald appeared. Tom took one basket, Rufus another. "Miss Green is back," announced Reginald. "I saw her car, just before that big streak of lightning."

"Let's go to Miss Green's house, instead of

our car," said Molly. For if they went to Miss Green's house, they could still have their picnic.

Mother was counting. "Nine children. You are all here," she said. "Yes, I think it's a good idea to go to Miss Green's house. I am sure she will let us picnic on her porch."

Rain was pounding on the roof of the neat white house by the time the Hubbard family had straggled up the hill. Miss Green met them at the door and welcomed them in. "I am so glad you have come to take shelter here," she said. "Sunday afternoons are usually so dull."

It was Miss Green who noticed that Edward was missing. That was when the picnic lunch had been spread out on a table and the smaller children were being served first. "Why, where is Edward?" she said. "Didn't he come with you?"

"Yes, Edward came," said Father. But where was Edward?

"I am sure I counted him," said Mother. But Edward was not there.

"Wasn't he with you, Molly?" asked Alicia, looking around in dismay.

Everyone looked at Molly, and Molly looked at the table, where there were so many delicious things. She couldn't eat the stuffed eggs now, or the cold sliced ham, because she was supposed to look after Edward. She couldn't bite into a sandwich, because Edward was lost and she didn't know when or how it had happened. "But you counted him," she said, looking tearfully at Mother.

"Cheer up, Molly, and eat your lunch," said Father. "Edward must have run straight to our car."

"I never thought of the car," said Mother. "Of course! He must be there."

Edward was not in the car, though. When the storm had passed, and Molly and Father set out to find him, they met him walking up the hillside from the brook. His face was serene and he was not wet at all.

"Where were you, Edward?" asked Father. "Didn't you hear us calling you?"

"No, I didn't," said Edward. "I was under the waterfall."

"Under the waterfall!" cried Molly. "Why didn't you get wet?"

"It wasn't raining under the waterfall," said Edward.

Father laughed. "You couldn't have found a dryer place," he said.

Edward had a special picnic all by himself, and while he ate, Miss Green hovered over him. "Poor Edward," she kept saying. But he didn't feel poor. There was a nice, dry rock under the waterfall and he had enjoyed sitting there with the storm all around him. "A waterfall is like a sort of umbrella," he said.

"But you must look after the twins next time," said Mother.

"I washed their faces," said Edward.

"That was early this morning."

When the Hubbard family and Becky were all driving home, Molly said, "I know why we didn't miss Edward. It was because of Becky."

"That's not polite," said Alicia.

"I mean, there were *ten* children on the picnic," said Molly.

"Molly is right," said Mother. "There were ten children, and I counted only nine!"

3

APPLE PIE AND CHOCOLATE CAKE

Alicia and Molly were on the front porch, minding John, when they saw Miss Wilson, a friend of Mother's, come walking down the street. There was nothing unusual about that except for one thing: Miss Wilson was carrying a big chocolate cake. "She is coming here," said Alicia, as Miss Wilson turned up their walk.

"Hello, girls," said Miss Wilson. "Is your mother at home? I have brought her a chocolate cake for the church sale tomorrow."

"It looks lovely," said Alicia. "Won't you sit down, Miss Wilson? Molly, please go and tell Mother that Miss Wilson is here."

You could almost always find Mother in the kitchen, which was in a wing at the back of the house. She was there this afternoon, cooking a fish chowder. Apple pies were in the oven and the kitchen was hot, but it was filled with delicious smells. Molly began to feel hungry as soon as she stepped into it.

"Miss Wilson is here, with a chocolate cake for the church sale," said Molly.

"A chocolate cake?" said Mother. "Oh, dear, she made a mistake. I asked her if she would make a coconut cake. But I won't say anything, because I don't want to hurt her feelings. Will you watch the pies, Molly, while I go and thank her?"

Mother whisked off her apron and went toward the front of the house, and Molly sat down on the kitchen stool to watch the pies. She felt a particular interest in the pies, because she had helped make them. She had peeled the apples, and when Mother had put on the top crusts, Molly had pricked an *A,* for *apple,* in the middle of each one. Just one pie was never enough for the Hubbard family. Mother always made three at a time except when there were guests, when she baked an extra one. Molly opened the oven door, to be sure all three pies were there. They were, and they looked very plump and juicy.

The kitchen door slammed open, and in came a twin. It slammed open again, and in marched the other. The two little boys both wanted to peek inside the oven, and Molly let them each have just one peek.

"I'm hungry," said the twin whose name was Gregory.

"I'm hungry too," said the twin whose name was Gordon. "What kind of pies are those, Molly?"

"Apple pies, and they are for supper. Run outdoors and play until suppertime," said Molly.

The twins went out, banging the door behind

them and singing a song about apple pies. A moment later, Edward appeared at the pantry door. "What did you say about pies?" he asked.

"I said that there were apple pies for supper," said Molly.

"Well, I like chocolate cake better," said Edward.

"Who told you about a chocolate cake?" asked Molly suspiciously.

"Nobody," said Edward, and went outdoors.

The pies were done now and so was the chowder, but Mother had not come back to the kitchen. Molly turned off the stove and went to look for her. As she passed through the hall the telephone rang, and she stopped to answer it. "Hello," she said.

"Hello," said Becky's voice. "Is that Molly? What time are you going to have supper?"

"Six o'clock as usual, I suppose," said Molly.

"Thank you," said Becky. "Alicia invited me to supper, but she didn't say what time."

Molly hung up the receiver and glanced into

the dining room, where a chocolate cake had been placed on the sideboard. It was the cake Miss Wilson had brought for the church sale, and Alicia must have put it there, out of reach of the twins. It was a delicious-looking cake, but Molly did not go near it. She went on down the hall and out to the porch, where she found Mother and Miss Wilson and Alicia. They were discussing the church sale, which seemed to be quite important. Mother and Miss Wilson were both on the sale committee, and Mother was the one in charge.

"The pies are done, Mother," said Molly softly.

"Pies?" asked Alicia. "What kind are they?"

The twins came running from the side yard, shouting, "Apple pies!"

"I am sure they are very good," murmured Miss Wilson. For Mother was famous for her apple pies.

"You must stay for supper and share some with us," said Mother, looking pleased.

But Molly could not help feeling disappointed when she heard Miss Wilson accepting Mother's invitation. She had helped make the apple pies, which were her favorite kind, and she knew that three were only enough for the family. There was not time for Mother to make another before supper, and now Miss Wilson was staying and Becky was coming. There won't be enough pie to go around, thought Molly. She felt still more anxious when Father telephoned to Mother to say that he was going to bring a friend home to supper!

In a short while a crowd had gathered on the Hubbard porch, for Becky had arrived, followed by the three big boys, who declared that they were as hungry as bears. Then Father came home from his office with his friend, Mr. Riverton, and Molly was sure that they were hungry too.

Mother called the girls aside. "Alicia, please talk to the guests," she said. "And Molly, please set the table for me." Molly went back to the kitchen with Mother. "Will there be enough to go around?" she asked.

"Oh, yes," said Mother, who was used to unexpected guests. "I made chowder, and there is some cold ham in the icebox."

"But what about the dessert?" asked Molly, thinking of the apple pies.

"Perhaps there won't be enough pie for everyone," said Mother. She hesitated. Then she said, "We could serve my chocolate cake, too. Will you put the cake on the sideboard?"

"It's already there," said Molly, feeling puzzled. She wondered what Miss Wilson would think when Mother served the cake she had brought. She did not know that Mother had also baked a chocolate cake, intended for the church sale tomorrow. She did not know that Mother's cake was on a shelf in the pantry. "What will Miss Wilson say?" she asked, before she went into the dining room.

"Miss Wilson won't even know," said Mother.

Feeling even more puzzled, Molly set the

table. She did not argue with her mother, who usually knew what was the best thing to do. Anyway, she thought, there would be plenty of apple pie, because every one of the boys preferred chocolate cake!

By the time the clock struck six o'clock, supper was ready, and Mother invited the guests into the dining room. John was already in his high chair, with a spoon in his hand, and all the other children were finding their places. Miss Wilson was given the seat of honor next to Father, while Mr. Riverton was seated next to Mother. Alicia and Becky sat side by side, next to the three big boys, and smiled across the table at Molly and Edward and the twins.

Molly smiled back. It was fun being in a large family and having guests for supper, and lots of good food. But while she was eating her chowder, her eyes kept straying to Miss Wilson's chocolate cake on the sideboard. Miss Wilson was going to be surprised, she was sure, when the time came for Father to cut that chocolate cake.

Alicia, who had put it there, never guessed that the cake was going to be passed around and eaten. She was busy carrying dishes out to the kitchen when Mother said, "Molly, will you put the cake on the table?"

Molly set the cake in front of Father.

"Yum yum," said one of the twins. "Chocolate cake!"

"I knew there was going to be chocolate cake," said Edward.

Miss Wilson, of course, said nothing. But Molly looked at her, and she did seem surprised.

When Alicia returned from the kitchen the cake had been cut. She looked at the sideboard and knew at once what had happened. "Oh, somebody made a mistake!" she cried. "That's the chocolate cake that Miss Wilson made for the sale."

"Oh, no," said Mother. But she took a closer look at the cake. It was not hers, and the plate it was on was not hers either. "I am so sorry," she said, turning to Miss Wilson. "You see, I made a chocolate cake too!"

Father and Mr. Riverton both laughed, for they thought that the cake mix-up was a good joke. Tom and Rufus and Reginald all laughed too. Since the cake was already cut, there was no reason for not eating it.

Molly was glad to see that Miss Wilson was smiling now. "Everyone makes mistakes sometimes," said Miss Wilson. "I have just remembered that I had promised to make a coconut cake—and I'll make one, the first thing in the morning."

Molly sighed with relief. She caught Mother's eye and smiled. Miss Wilson's feelings weren't hurt, and there was enough apple pie. She wished, though, that she had known about the cake Mother had made. If she had, there wouldn't have been any mix-up at all. Suddenly a thought darted into Molly's mind: Edward must have known about Mother's cake all along. She pounced on him after supper and said, "Did you see Mother's cake?"

"I saw a cake way up on the pantry shelf," said Edward.

4

THE CANOE TRIP

Molly had had a letter from her friend Carol, telling about the fun she was having at camp. The letter made Molly wish that she could go to camp too, and she asked her father and mother if they would send her to the camp where Carol was.

"I'm afraid not," said Mother. "Camps are rather expensive."

"You see, Molly, it's this way," said Father. "If we sent you to camp, Alicia would want to go; and if you and Alicia were both at a girls' camp, all the boys—except John—would want to go to a boys' camp."

"I see," said Molly. If eight boys and girls all went to camp it certainly would be expensive. Carol was an only child, which was why she could go. "Camping would be fun, though," said Molly.

Father and Mother agreed that camping was fun. However, there were other things to do in the summer that were just as much fun, they said—canoeing, for instance. "How would you like to go on a canoe trip?" asked Father.

Of course Molly wanted to go, and of course the other children said that they wanted to go on a canoe trip too. "I won't jiggle the canoe," Edward promised.

"Gordon and I won't jiggle either," chimed in Gregory.

Mother looked at Father and shook her head. "I think the twins had better stay at home with me," she said. "They don't know how to swim yet, and canoes are tippy things."

"I know how to swim, though," said Edward.

That was true. Edward could swim six strokes. Father said that he would take him on the canoe trip. Edward would be the youngest one, so Father himself would watch him. "You won't be Molly's responsibility this time," he said.

One nice thing about the town where the Hubbards lived was the Outing Club, which Father belonged to. There were several cabins within hiking distance of the town that were owned and kept up by the Outing Club. There was even one cabin on an island in the river, and a trip to the island cabin was what Father had planned. It would be the next best thing to camping, for they could take provisions and cook in the cabin.

The members of the Outing Club had keys to a boathouse, where twelve canoes owned by the club were kept. Father had a key, and this meant that he could take out a canoe whenever he wished. He could take out more than one canoe if he needed more than one. "And we'll need two canoes," he said, after counting the children. Besides the three boys and Alicia, Molly, and Edward, a friend of Tom's named Hunter was going on the trip. Hunter was a tall, strong boy who knew how to paddle, and he had often been to the island before. He and Tom would be in charge of one canoe, and Father and Rufus would be in charge of the other.

On Saturday morning the party assembled down by the boathouse. Molly watched Father and the boys lift two canoes from their racks and push them, prows forward, into the river. She helped Alicia put the provisions in each of the canoes, and then she climbed into the one that Father was going to steer.

"Now, Edward," said Father. But Edward paused. He didn't want to get into Father's canoe; he wanted to get into Hunter's. He had heard his brothers saying how well Hunter could paddle, and he wanted to be in the canoe that reached the island first. "I would like to go in the other canoe," he said to Father.

"It's already full," said Father. For Alicia and Reginald were in the other canoe, which Hunter was shoving off from the shore. "I'll come with you, Father," said Edward hastily, not wanting to be left behind.

The river was beautiful, with its green, wooded shores reflected upside down in the water. The slender, green-painted canoes were beautiful too. Molly wished that she could go canoeing every day. The canoes skimmed downstream, helped by the swift current. As the river curved, a small green island came into view. "Look! There is the island already," Molly cried.

But Father said, "That is not the island with a cabin, Molly. Don't you know that the river is dotted with islands? That island ahead of us is just the first dot."

"Oh," said Molly.

"That is just a dot," said Edward. "The island we are going to is Hunter's Island, because he has been there before."

The other canoe was ahead, for it had started first. It seemed to be getting farther and farther away, and Edward wished that Father and Rufus would paddle faster. Father, in the stern, was keeping time with Rufus; and Rufus, in the prow, was paddling with all his might. But he was not as strong as either Tom or Hunter, and when Edward urged him to go faster and catch up with the others, he said, "You try and paddle a canoe someday, Edward. It isn't quite as easy as it looks."

The island with a cabin was far down the river. Molly counted three more bends and two more islets before she saw a larger island rising from the water. A call floated back from Tom, "Island ahoy," and Molly knew that this island was more than a dot.

As Father steered the canoe closer, Molly saw the cabin. It looked to her scarcely larger than a dollhouse. "They got there first," said Edward, for the other canoe was landing. "When we go back, may I be in Hunter's canoe?" he asked.

"I don't see why not, if you sit still," said Father.

The island cabin was really much bigger than a dollhouse. Molly went with Alicia to inspect it right away. They were charmed to find a kerosene lamp and a wood-burning stove, and they liked the thick, white cups and plates, which were different from Mother's.

"This is like a camp," said Molly.

"And I am the camp cook," said Alicia. "You can help me, Molly, because Edward is with Father."

"He couldn't get lost on an island, anyway," said Molly, as she set cups and plates on the table.

Nothing ever tasted quite so good to Molly as the meal she helped Alicia cook on the wood stove that day. They did not have to call Father and the boys to dinner, for they all flocked into the cabin to eat the steak and onions and the platterful of fried potatoes.

Edward sat next to Hunter, and all that afternoon he did not stray far from his side. Hunter was good to Edward; he answered his questions and treated him as though he were as old as himself.

Before it was time to start for home, everyone went swimming, and Edward showed off his six strokes to Hunter. His older brothers were all diving from the canoes. "Come on, Edward, let's see you dive," said Reginald.

"I'm swimming," said Edward, splashing after Hunter.

"Yes, we see you swimming," said Rufus. "How about a dive?"

"Not now," said Edward. He had come to the end of his six strokes, and he caught hold of Father. Molly was glad that it was not up to her to keep him from sinking.

And Molly was very glad that she did not have to look out for Edward on the homeward trip. He was not in Father's canoe this time; he was in Hunter's. Father's canoe had a head start, but Hunter paddled faster, and Edward waved gaily as he sped past Molly.

"Edward must be happy now," said Alicia,

who had taken Edward's place in Father's canoe.

"What are they doing now?" asked Molly, turning to look.

"They are changing places," said Rufus, from his seat in the prow.

"Tom ought to know better," said Father. "They will upset the canoe."

What had happened was that Edward kept teasing to paddle, and Hunter had said to Tom, "Let him try for a while." Paddling in the prow is easier than in the stern, so Tom, who was in the prow, replied, "All right. He can take my place."

"Move," said Reginald.

Edward stood up.

"Take my hand," said Tom.

Edward took his hand.

"Don't tip the canoe," warned Reginald. The canoe wobbled a bit, but Edward managed to change places with Tom safely.

To the surprise of the older boys, Edward paddled quite well. He didn't say a word, and he didn't even smile. As far as Edward was concerned, the canoe was his; it was a birch-bark canoe, and he was an Indian.

When the two canoes had almost reached the boathouse landing, Father called, "Good for you, Edward! I have been watching you."

"I can paddle," said Edward briefly. "I can dive, too."

"Oh!" cried Molly, as Edward plunged headfirst into the water.

"Oh!" cried Alicia, as Father dived in after him.

But Father did not really need to dive in after Edward. Edward's six strokes carried him to the shore.

"It was quite a trip," Molly told Mother as soon as she reached home. "You should have seen Edward!"

"What did he do?" asked Mother.

"You'd better ask Father," Molly said. She felt quite proud of Edward—but how glad she was that she had not had charge of him today!

5

EXACTLY LIKE MOTHER

Since there were so many Hubbards, their relatives often sent them boxes of clothes which they thought might be useful. The two girls were the ones who liked to open the boxes, for they were interested in trying on clothes. Hats, gloves, dresses, and jackets—you never could tell what wonders a box might hold. There were boys' clothes, too, of course; but they were not pretty, and Alicia and Molly had no use for them.

One day when a box of clothes arrived, Mother told the girls to open it and try on anything they liked. She was going to a club meeting that afternoon, and she did not have time to sort clothes first.

It was a rainy day, and the house was filled with children. Tom and Rufus and Reginald were all in Tom's room, working on some kind of machine. They had shut Edward out, so he was playing with the twins. Edward had made a tent in the hall with two chairs and a blanket, for he was being an Indian and the twins were cowboys.

"Play nicely," Mother said, as she left the house.

Molly looked after her wistfully. She wished she could be grown-up like Mother and go to club meetings without children tagging along. "Don't make so much noise, Edward," she said. "No, you must not let Hugo in." For Hugo was not allowed in the house.

"He's an Indian dog," said Edward.

"He's an Irish setter," said Molly.

"But he is my dog, and I am an Indian," said Edward.

Molly could see that Edward was just being tiresome. She started up the stairs, where she met John, who was climbing slowly down, step by step. Alicia was supposed to be taking care of John, but she was showing Becky what was inside the box that had arrived that day.

Molly picked up John and joined Becky and Alicia. "Here is John, Alicia," she said. "Do you know where I found him? He was going downstairs all by himself."

"That's all he wants to do, all day long," said Alicia. "He was here with me just a second ago. Look, Molly! See all the things that came in the box. There are some ladies' dresses this time."

"I want to try on one of the ladies' dresses," said Molly.

The three girls each picked out a beautiful dress, and twirled around in front of the long mirror in Mother's room. The dresses were too big for them, but they didn't mind that. "I look like a real lady," said Becky, who had chosen an evening gown.

"But look at Molly," said Alicia. "Molly looks just like Mother."

Molly smiled at her reflection. She did look like her mother. The flowered dress she had picked out was like one that Mother wore, and since it trailed to the floor it made Molly seem quite tall. "I'll pin up your hair," said Alicia, and she pinned Molly's braids around her head, like Mother's. "Now, look at yourself."

"How do you do, Mrs. Hubbard?" said Becky, holding out her hand.

There was a clatter on the stairs, and a twin came running into the room, banging the door behind him. "Edward says I have to be a squaw!" he cried. "I don't want to be a squaw, because squaws are girls."

"You don't have to be a squaw unless you want to," said Alicia. "Where is Edward?"

"Here I am," said Edward, opening the door. "I've got a lasso, and I'm going to lasso somebody."

Becky gathered her skirts around her and climbed up on the bed. "Make him stop! I don't want to be lassoed," she cried.

"Go away, Edward. Go away, Twin," said Alicia.

"Mother told you to play nicely when she left," said Molly.

"Lassos are nice," said Edward. "Look out, Molly!"

"You won't lasso me," said Molly, and slipped past him to the hall. Alicia would make Edward and the twins behave, she thought, and now was her chance to be alone for a while. She decided to go up on the widow's walk and see if the rain had stopped.

The way to the widow's walk was through the attic. Molly tiptoed up the stairs so that nobody would hear her. She stumbled once on her trailing skirt and then went quietly through the trap door that led to the widow's walk. She left it open, so that she could get down again. The rain had stopped, and a rainbow arched across the sky. Molly climbed up on the railing and looked out at the town. The streets were wet and shining. Down the gleaming sidewalk came the minister of the church the Hubbard family went to. He happened to look up as he passed the Hubbard house, and he saw the figure perched on the railing of the widow's walk.

Perhaps the minister was rather nearsighted, or perhaps Molly really looked grown-up in the long dress, with her hair pinned on top of her head. Whichever it was, he touched his hat, and said, "Good afternoon," as if Molly were her mother!

Molly smiled delightedly. She did look like Mother! Feeling as grown-up as could be, she replied, "Good afternoon, Mr. Martin. I certainly enjoyed your sermon last Sunday."

It seemed to Molly that Mr. Martin looked pleased. However, her feeling of dignity quickly vanished when Edward climbed through the trap door that she had left open. A happy bark could be heard as Hugo followed Edward. He had been let into the house, after

all. "Down, Hugo!" cried Molly, for Hugo bounded toward her and almost knocked her off her perch.

"We found you!" "We heard you!" Here came the twins. Molly looked anxiously at the sidewalk below, to see if Mr. Martin had heard the commotion on the roof. But he had passed by. Molly sighed, for she had wanted to act like Mother a little while longer. It was no fun on the widow's walk with a whole menagerie, so she said, "I am going downstairs to see what Alicia is doing. Come on, all of you, and put Hugo outdoors."

John was sitting in the tent that Edward had made, Becky had gone home, and Alicia was rather cross. "Where have you been?" she said, as soon as she saw Molly. "You shouldn't have gone off and left me with all those children. Sometimes you don't act a bit grown-up."

"I can act exactly like Mother," said Molly.

But while Molly was changing back into her own dress, a thought suddenly came to her that made her feel worried. Mother never, *never* went up on the roof, and Mother never, *never* climbed up on railings! If Mr. Martin had really thought that she was Mother he must have wondered why she was in such a queer place.

I'll have to explain, thought Molly. And when she saw Mother coming home from her club meeting, she ran down the street. She slipped her hand in Mother's and said, "If you see Mr. Martin, please tell him that I am the person he saw up on the widow's walk."

"I will, Molly," said Mother. "Who did he think it was?"

"You," said Molly.

"Gracious!" said Mother. "He must have thought that I had grown very small."

"Oh, no," said Molly. "I was looking very tall, because I was wearing a lady's dress that came in the box."

"But I never go up on the roof," said Mother. And Molly still felt worried, for she was a conscientious little girl.

A few days later Mr. Martin came to call, and Molly heard him say to Mother, "Your daughter Molly is growing so fast that the other day I thought she was you for a moment."

Molly listened, wondering what he would say next.

"But I looked again, and saw that I was mistaken," said Mr. Martin. "The three little boys and the big dog were with her, as usual." He did not mention the widow's walk, but even so, Molly felt quite grateful to Edward and the twins.

6

THE BENNINGTON BABY

The Hubbard children all helped take care of John, but Alicia was the only one who took care of other babies. Quite often the telephone rang, and a neighbor asked Alicia if she could come and stay with her baby that night. Alicia generally said yes. She did not mind staying in somebody else's house, guarding a sleeping baby. If the baby woke up and cried, she knew how to hush it to sleep again; and she knew how to warm a bottle if the baby was hungry.

When a baby's parents were planning to stay out late, they would tell Alicia, and she would bring her nightgown and toothbrush and go to bed in the guest room when she got sleepy. Otherwise, she would bring a book, and read until the parents came back. One of them always offered to take her safely home.

One day a rather new neighbor called up and asked if Alicia could come and stay with her baby. "The call is for you, Alicia," said Mother, who had answered the phone. "Mrs. Bennington wants you to stay with her baby tonight, because she and her husband are going to a dance."

This time Alicia said no. Becky and her big sister had asked her to go to the movies with them. "Can't Molly go to the Benningtons' instead of me?" she said.

"I don't see why not," said Mother. "Would you like to go and stay with the Bennington baby, Molly?"

Molly's face glowed. "I'd love to," she said. She had seen the Bennington baby on the lawn in a play pen. It was a girl baby, and Molly liked girl babies. She often wished she had a baby sister. "Shall I take my nightgown and toothbrush, like Alicia?" she asked.

"We'll see," said Mother. Then she asked Mrs. Bennington if she would mind having Molly in Alicia's place. "Of course not," said Mrs. Bennington. "We will not be very late, but if Molly gets sleepy she can sleep in the guest room."

When Molly had finished her supper she set out for the Benningtons' house, which was up one block and down another. She carried her toothbrush rolled in her nightgown, and she repeated to herself all the instructions her mother had given her. "Telephone me if you get lonely," Mother had said. "And telephone me if you don't know what to do." But Molly felt sure that she would know exactly what to do. Hadn't she often taken care of John?

Mr. and Mrs. Bennington were a very young couple. Their house was pretty and new, and so was their baby, who was a good deal younger than John. As Molly went up the walk, Mrs. Bennington opened the door. "I am so glad you have come, Molly," she said. "Barbara is being naughty, but since you have a baby brother, perhaps you will know how to quiet her." Loud yells came from upstairs.

Molly followed Mrs. Bennington up to the nursery, where Barbara stood in her crib, shaking its railing. Her hair was tousled and she was quite red in the face. "Isn't she terrible?" said Mrs. Bennington. "She always acts like this when we are going out."

"She's a real little tyrant," said Mr. Bennington, coming into the room. The two parents stood side by side, looking at Molly as though they expected her to do something.

Molly did not know Barbara, but she knew what John liked. John liked very simple games. She walked over to Barbara's crib and knelt beside it. "Boo," she said softly, through the bars.

Barbara stopped crying. She dropped down in her crib and stared at Molly with round, astonished eyes. Then she put one hand between the bars and touched Molly's face. "Boo," she said sweetly.

"I can see you will be a good baby watcher," said Mr. Bennington.

"She's a lovely baby," said Molly.

"Sometimes," said Mrs. Bennington. "But sometimes she's bad. I would give her away, any time!"

When the Benningtons had left and Barbara had gone to sleep, Molly thought over what Mrs. Bennington had said. It was very quiet in the house, with only the sound of a clock ticking. She had not brought a book to read, and the books in this house looked dull. Did Mrs. Bennington really mean what she said about Barbara? Molly wondered. Grown-up people often made jokes that were hard to understand. But was Mrs. Bennington joking? Molly did not know. She supposed that some people liked babies more than others did, and she thought that perhaps Mrs. Bennington was tired of her baby.

Then Molly remembered how she had seen the Bennington baby sitting in a play pen, all by herself. If her mother really wanted her, wouldn't she play with her? John had never been left alone in his life. Molly tiptoed up the stairs to look at Barbara, who was just like a doll when she was asleep. She wished that she had a little sister exactly like Barbara. In fact, she wished that she had Barbara!

When Molly went downstairs again she telephoned Mother. "Hello," said Mother. "Are you lonely, Molly?"

"Not very," said Molly. "But, oh, Mother! Mrs. Bennington doesn't seem to want her baby."

"Nonsense," said Mother. "I don't believe that."

"But she said she would like to give her away."

"She was joking," said Mother. "You had better go to sleep now, Molly, because it is getting late."

Molly looked at the clock that ticked so

loudly. It said half past ten, but Molly did not feel sleepy. She did not want to go to bed in somebody else's house. She curled up in an armchair and thought about Barbara, while the clock ticked on and on.

Molly must have fallen asleep, for when she looked up it was half past eleven, and Barbara was crying. She flew upstairs to the nursery and lifted her out of the crib. Barbara sighed, and clasped her arms around Molly's neck.

She likes me, and her parents don't want her, thought Molly. Mother was wrong, because Mrs. Bennington wasn't joking. They haven't come back from the dance yet, and they said they would be early. "Sh–h–h, Barbara," she said aloud. "I will take you home with me." For that was what she had decided to do.

The light on the Hubbard porch was shining, but the rest of the house was dark except for the hall, where a night light burned. All the family had gone to bed, since it was nearly midnight. Molly, with Barbara in her arms,

went softly up the stairs. She had thought of putting Barbara in her own bed, but she shared a room with Alicia, and Alicia might wake up. She went to John's room instead, and laid Barbara beside John. Barbara had gone to sleep again, and John did not stir.

A short time later the telephone rang. It woke her father and mother, but it did not wake Molly, who was fast asleep in her own bed. "Hello," said Father, picking up the receiver. "What? Your baby? I can't believe it."

But Mother was at his elbow. "Molly said something about Mrs. Bennington's not wanting her baby," she whispered. "She was supposed to spend the night at the Benningtons'. But do you think she could have come home, bringing the baby with her?"

"That's what they say," said Father.

Together they went to the girls' room, and there was Molly; but there was no sign of the Bennington baby. Mother sighed with relief, but Father said, "Wait. If the baby is not at their house it *must* be here."

By the time Father and Mother had discovered Barbara, the front doorbell was ringing loudly. It pealed through the house, waking Alicia, who woke Molly. "Who can be here in the middle of the night, Molly?" she said.

Molly's heart gave a thump. She was out of bed in a minute. "I think Mr. and Mrs. Bennington may be here," she whispered.

"Why, you have a dress on! Where is your nightgown?" said Alicia.

"I left it at the Benningtons' house, and my toothbrush, too," said Molly.

Mr. and Mrs. Bennington had come to claim their baby. Molly, from the head of the stairs, saw Mother in the hall, handing Barbara to Mrs. Bennington. Mrs. Bennington hugged Barbara as though she really loved her. Molly walked slowly down the stairs.

"Oh, Molly!" said Mother.

Molly looked at Mrs. Bennington. "You said you would give her away."

"I was only joking. Didn't you know that?" said Mrs. Bennington.

Molly shook her head, but said nothing.

When Mr. and Mrs. Bennington had taken Barbara home, Molly began to cry. Mother tried to comfort her. "Never mind, Molly. You just didn't understand," she said.

"I do understand, perfectly well," sobbed Molly. "But I wish we could have kept Barbara!"

"I can't understand *you,* Molly," said Father, shaking his head. "Nine children in the family ought to be enough!"

7

LEMONADE FOR SALE

It was a hot afternoon, and Molly, in her prettiest dress, was sitting on the front steps. She had been invited to a birthday party in the next block, but Edward and the twins were not invited and Molly was in charge of them until Mother came home.

"I wish Mother would hurry up," she said to Edward. Mother had gone to lunch with a friend, taking Alicia and John with her. She had told Molly they would be back by three o'clock, but it was half past three now and they had not returned.

"I wish I could go to Main Street and buy an ice-cream cone," said Edward. "I wish I were rich, like Tom and Rufus and Reginald."

The three big boys always had money in their pockets, for they all had odd jobs during the summer. Alicia was paid when she took care of babies, so she had money too. Molly sighed. She did not think she would ever be asked again to stay with the Bennington baby, or anyone else's.

This afternoon the three big boys had all gone off, leaving Edward behind as usual. They had ridden away on their bicycles to play ball with their friends, and they had not wanted to bother with a little brother.

"It isn't fair," said Edward.

Molly knew what he meant. It wasn't fair for the big boys to leave him behind. She did not mind—so very much—missing the birthday party. Her best friend, Carol, was still away at camp, and her second-best friend, Sarah, was still in the mountains. This party was being given by Millicent, her third-best friend, and Millicent's parties were never very lively. Still, there would surely be ice cream and cake, and a big pitcher of cold lemonade.

The twins were riding their tricycles up and down the sidewalk. They went as far as the corner and then came back again, because they were not allowed to cross Elm Street. Cars went fast on Elm Street, which turned into a highway as soon as it left the town. Edward was counting the cars. "Sixteen," he announced. "I have counted sixteen cars going by."

Molly wondered where all the people in all the cars were going, and if they were as hot and thirsty as she was. She decided to go into the house and make some lemonade while she was waiting for Mother. No sooner had she decided that than another idea came to her: she and Edward could sell lemonade! They could carry a table out to the corner of Elm Street and put the pitcher there, and some paper cups.

Surely some of the people who were traveling through the town would want to stop and buy a cup of cold lemonade.

"Let's sell lemonade," she said.

"Who will buy it?" asked Edward.

"Travelers passing by," said Molly.

Edward's face lighted up. "Let's," he said. "We can make money, just like Tom and Rufus and Reginald."

Molly went into the kitchen, where she found some lemons. There were a lot—enough to make a bucketful of lemonade. A bucket would hold more than a pitcher, so Molly put ice in a bucket. Selling lemonade was a good idea, she thought.

Molly squeezed lemons, and squeezed more lemons. When Edward came into the kitchen to see if the lemonade was ready, she had made a bucketful and was filling a pitcher besides. "See if you can find a small table," she told Edward.

"What for?" said Edward.

"For a lemonade stand," said Molly.

Edward went off, and while Molly was taking paper cups out of a drawer he returned, with the smallest table he could find. "Will this be all right?" he asked. Molly nodded.

Gordon and Gregory and the Irish setter, Hugo, were all very much interested in what happened next. The twins stopped riding their tricycles and trailed behind Edward as he carried the table to the corner of Elm Street. As for Hugo, he followed closely at Molly's heels as she carried the bucketful of lemonade. Another trip would have to be made for the pitcher and the cups. "There," said Molly, setting the bucket down on the grass, since it was too heavy for the little table. "Keep away, Hugo. That lemonade's not for you."

Off she hurried to the kitchen, to fetch the cups and the pitcher. When she came back, Hugo was lapping thirstily from the bucket!

"Bad dog, Hugo!" Molly cried. Then she turned to the twins. "Why did you let Hugo drink the lemonade?"

"He was thirsty," said Gordon.

"But the lemonade is for sale—and nobody will want a drink from that bucket now," said Molly.

"I do," said Gregory, reaching for a cup.

"You mustn't," said Molly. "Where is Edward?" For Hugo was Edward's dog, and it was up to Edward to make his dog behave.

"Here I am," said Edward. "The cars won't stop." He had been waving to each car as it passed, hoping that someone would want to buy lemonade.

Since Hugo had been drinking the lemonade in the bucket, Molly said that he might as well have the rest of it. The pitcher and the cups, she arranged on the table. "Now, everybody behave," she said.

"But I want some lemonade," said Gordon.

"So do I," said Gregory.

Molly let the twins each have one cupful from the pitcher. She drank some too, and so did Edward. "We will have to sell the rest to make some money," she said. But the cars kept passing by without stopping.

"When people sell things they have signs," Edward remarked.

That was true, Molly agreed. They ought to have a sign. But she did not want to go back to the house again. She didn't trust Hugo, and she didn't want to leave her stand, with everything so carefully arranged. "Can you make a sign, Edward?" she asked. "You know how to print *Lemonade for Sale, 5 Cents a Cup,* don't you?"

Edward said yes, and went back toward the house.

It seemed to Molly that Edward was gone for a long time; she wondered if he were having trouble finding a piece of cardboard. She wished she had told him about the cardboard in Father's clean shirts, which had come back from the laundry that morning. The twins rode off around the block on their tricycles, not telling Molly where they were going, and Molly waited patiently by the lemonade stand. Nobody passed by, and still Mother did not come home.

Before the next car passed, bicycle bells rang, and Tom and Rufus and Reginald came riding along the street. They all three swerved, and came to a stop as soon as they saw Molly. "What have you got there, Molly?" asked Tom.

"Lemonade," said Molly.

Lemonade! All the boys wanted some.

"You have to pay for it," said Molly.

"We can pay," said Reginald. "How much is it?"

"A nickel a cup," said Molly.

The boys fished in their pockets. They had nickels, and dimes, too. They were thirsty as well as rich, for they drank a lot of lemonade. They drank cupful after cupful, until the pitcher was empty and there was a pile of nickels and dimes on the table.

Molly felt half pleased and half disappointed. It was lucky for her that her three big brothers had come to her rescue and bought the lemonade that she had made. On the other hand, it would have been more exciting to have sold it to strangers passing through the town.

There was a pocket in Molly's dress. She put the money in it and carried the empty pitcher back to the house. She called to Edward, but he did not answer her; Molly thought that he must have forgotten all about the sign. There was no use in making one now, anyway, since there were no more lemons. Molly went back for the table and was just taking it home when Mother drove up, with Alicia and John.

"Oh, Molly, I am sorry we are late," said Mother. "Put down that table and run along to Millicent's party."

"What were you doing with that table?" asked Alicia.

"I was selling lemonade," said Molly.

"Did Edward and the twins help?" asked Alicia.

"No," said Molly. She looked up and down the sidewalk, but the twins were not in sight. "They all went off," she added.

"Never mind. Alicia can look for them while you go to the party," said Mother.

But Molly was the one who found Edward and the twins. For when she came to Millicent's house, there they all were, playing amidst a flock of children on the lawn! All three wore fancy paper hats, each one had a balloon, and Hugo, who had come to the party too, was making it the liveliest party Millicent had ever had.

I might have guessed that they were all here, thought Molly. She was very cross with them and a bit cross with herself, for not having come to the party sooner.

"Hello, Molly," said Edward.

When Molly did not answer, he said, "I didn't make any sign. You see, I thought that I had better look after the twins."

"But you weren't invited," whispered Molly.

That did not seem to trouble Millicent, though. She ran up to Molly and took hold of her hand. "I'm so glad you came to my party at last," she said. "I saved a paper hat for you and there is some lemonade."

Molly felt in her pocket where the dimes

and nickels were. They were all hers—not Edward's or the twins'. She put on the hat Millicent had saved for her and joined in the party, but she did not care about having even one glass of lemonade!

8

GUESTS IN THE PINK ROOM

One morning at the breakfast table Mother said, "What do you think, children? We are going to have some visitors."

"Who?" asked Alicia.

"For how long?" asked Molly.

"I hope they aren't going to sleep in my room," said Edward, for the last overnight guest had been put in Edward's room and he had been moved in with the twins.

There was no regular guest room in the

Hubbard house; the one that had once been the spare room belonged to the twins. Whenever any visitors came, the family had to decide which one of the bedrooms should be turned into a guest room. The three big boys never had to move out for a guest. They slept in three small bedrooms above the kitchen, which Mother did not consider good enough for guests, although the boys liked them.

The guests who were coming now were old friends, Mother told the children. They were Mr. and Mrs. Austin. "Father and I have not seen them since Tom was a baby, because they moved to Florida," she said.

"Have they got any children?" asked Molly.

"No," replied Mother. "When we saw them last," she added with a smile, "Tom howled all the time. They will be here in three days, so please take care of each other and have your best company manners."

"Which room is going to be the guest room?" was the next question.

"I had thought of giving Mr. and Mrs.

Austin the pink room, if you girls don't mind," said Mother.

Molly looked at Alicia, because she shared the pink room with her. It had got its name because of its pink-and-white-striped wallpaper. Molly liked sleeping in her own bed, the twin of Alicia's, and she did not feel like moving out for unknown guests, even though they were old friends of Mother and Father's.

"The guests can have my room," said Edward suddenly.

"Thank you, Edward," said Mother. "But your room is small, and I think they would be more comfortable in the pink room."

"But I want to sleep outdoors in the tent," said Edward.

"I will ask Becky if I can stay at her house," said Alicia.

Mother looked relieved. "It is all settled," she said. "If Alicia stays with Becky and Edward sleeps in the tent, Molly can have Edward's room and the Austins can have the pink room."

"I never stayed in a tent all night," said Edward happily.

"Well, it's waterproof, and I'll give you plenty of blankets," said Mother.

During the next three days the silver was shined, the floors were waxed, and the windows were washed. Mrs. Meek, who helped Mother out at special times, came all three days and polished and scrubbed. By the afternoon of the third day, the house was shiny-bright. Molly walked through it cautiously. It seemed to her as if the guests must be a king and queen, because of all the preparations.

When Father drove to the station to meet Mr. and Mrs. Austin, he took the twins along, because they begged to go with him. Molly waited on the porch with Mother and Alicia. She felt quite eager by this time to meet the guests. "Are Mr. and Mrs. Austin very grand?" she asked Mother.

"They are just old friends, as I told you," said Mother.

They must be very fussy old friends, thought

Molly, to have so much fuss made for them.

The old friends looked tired when they arrived. They had had a long, hot trip all the way from Florida. The twins had been sitting on their laps during the ride from the station, and Molly could tell right away that they were not used to children. Mrs. Austin seemed relieved when Gordon bounced out of the car, and Mr. Austin almost shoved Gregory off his knee.

Dinner that night was a great success, though. Every one of the nine children had company manners. They let the four grown-ups talk without interrupting them, and they did not reach for things on the table. When Edward took too big a mouthful, Molly kicked him gently; and when Reginald sneezed, Rufus nudged him. And Tom, who had howled during the Austins' last visit, cleared the table between courses and brought the dessert in.

The whole visit might have been a great success if Edward had not gone to sleep in his own bed that night, instead of going out to the tent.

After dinner, while Father and Mother were talking to their friends, Molly appeared in the doorway.

"What is it, Molly?" Mother asked.

"It's about Edward," said Molly. "He forgot he was going to spend the night outdoors in the tent, and he is sound asleep."

"Can't you wake him up?" said Mother.

"I tried to," said Molly.

Mother went upstairs with Molly and looked at Edward, who was much too fast asleep to be disturbed. "Would you mind sleeping in the tent, instead of Edward?" asked Mother. "Father put a mattress in it, and there are lots of blankets."

"No, I don't mind," said Molly. It might be fun to sleep in a tent. Alicia had already gone to Becky's house for the night, so Molly got ready for bed, put on her dressing gown, and went out to the back yard. There was a fingernail moon above the apple tree, and there were many twinkling stars.

Molly was half asleep when Hugo came into

the tent and lay down on the foot of the mattress. Hugo's bed was an old horse blanket on the back porch, but he preferred a softer spot whenever he could find one. He sighed with contentment. "Good dog," murmured Molly. She had left the flap of the tent open in order to see the stars, but she was asleep almost at once.

It must have been about midnight when Molly woke up. Her feet were cold, and she found that Hugo had pulled the covers off her and was curled up on top of them. "Bad dog," she said, pushing him away. She tried to cover herself again, but the blankets were in a tangle, and soggy with the damp night air.

The stars were shining brightly, but Molly was tired of spending the night outdoors. Edward was the one who had wanted to sleep in the tent, and he ought to be out here instead of her, she thought—especially since Hugo was his dog.

I am going to go and *make* Edward wake up, thought Molly. It was time for him to change

places with her. She ran across the dewy grass to the back door of the house, and Hugo uncurled himself and bounded after her.

Dogs have a way, sometimes, of slipping into a house as soon as anyone opens a door. Molly had no idea that Hugo had slipped into the kitchen with her until she heard him padding after her up the back stairs. She knew that it was useless to tell him to go back, for Hugo minded no one but Edward. She did not worry, though. If she managed to wake up Edward, Hugo would follow him back to the tent.

Everybody in the house was fast asleep. Molly went quietly into Edward's room. He looked very warm and cosy with his covers tucked around him—but it was certainly his turn to sleep in the tent.

"Wake up, Edward," said Molly.

Edward turned over.

"Get up, Edward," said Molly. "Look, here is Hugo."

At the mention of his name, Hugo stood on

his hind legs, put his paws on the bed, and licked Edward's face.

At that, Edward woke up. "What's the matter?" he said. He smiled at Molly and Hugo. "I thought that you were burglars."

"Don't talk so loud," whispered Molly. "Don't you remember that you were going to sleep in the tent?"

Edward shook his head, for he was still almost asleep.

"Get up. You have got to change places with me," said Molly.

At last Edward seemed to understand what she was saying, for he tumbled out of bed and started for the door. Molly jumped in the bed and burrowed under the covers. How nice and warm it was after the chilly tent!

A few seconds later, a piercing scream came from the pink room, where Mr. and Mrs. Austin had been peacefully sleeping. Mother woke up and so did Father. Lights were switched on and padding footsteps sounded through the upstairs hall.

Molly lay in bed, shivering. What had happened? she wondered. Could there possibly have been burglars in the house? Then she heard Mother say, "Edward! What have you been doing?" And she heard Father say, "Who let Hugo in?"

Molly, wide awake now, went out into the hall.

What had happened was that Edward had not gone to the tent, but had run straight to Molly's bed in the pink room. He had thought that all he was doing was changing places with Molly, for he had forgotten about Mr. and Mrs. Austin.

It was bad enough that Edward had startled Mr. Austin when he climbed into Molly's bed, which he thought was empty. But it was worse when Hugo had jumped on Alicia's bed. That was when Mrs. Austin had screamed so loudly.

Mr. and Mrs. Austin were not used to children and they were not used to dogs, either. It was too late to explain that Hugo was not allowed in the house; and they could not understand about Molly and the tent, or why Edward had rushed into their room at midnight.

Their visit was a short one. The next afternoon Father drove Mr. and Mrs. Austin to the station, leaving the twins behind this time. "Our guests didn't stay very long," said Alicia, who had missed all the excitement.

"No. They had promised to visit some other old friends," said Mother.

Molly wondered if the other old friends had a guest room, or if the Austins would have to sleep in somebody else's room. She felt rather sorry for them, although they certainly were fussy. After all, Edward and Hugo were not burglars!

9

EDWARD DISAPPEARS

Nine children were a lot for one father and mother, and Molly could not blame her parents when they wanted to go on a week-end trip by themselves. "We shall only be away two days," Mother told the children.

"Where are you going?" asked Alicia.

"To the White Mountains."

"When?" asked Molly.

"This next week end."

Now it happened that the three big boys had

been invited to go on a hiking trip that same week end. Their friend Hunter's father was taking them all to an Outing Club cabin not far away. "Which cabin?" asked Father, when he heard about their trip.

"Bear Cabin," said Tom. "Have you ever been there?"

Father said yes. It was on Hunters Hill.

Edward pricked up his ears. "Hunter's hill?" he asked. "Does it belong to Hunter, like Hunter's cabin?"

"Hunter hasn't got any cabin, or any hill. It just happens to be the same name," said Tom.

Mother had asked Mrs. Meek to come and keep house for the children while she and Father were away. It was lucky, she said, that the three big boys would be away too, for that would mean less work for Mrs. Meek. Mother and Father drove off early in the morning. They promised to telephone from the mountains that same evening, but they both felt sure that their nine children would be all right.

Mrs. Meek came to keep house. The three

big boys hurried through breakfast, eager to get started on their trip. They put knapsacks on their backs filled with things that they would need, for they were planning to stay at the cabin overnight. Molly and Edward watched them march off down the street. The house would seem very strange, thought Molly, with Mrs. Meek in the kitchen, and Father and Mother and the big boys all away at once. There are only six of us now, she thought, not counting Mrs. Meek.

"It isn't fair," said Edward.

"What isn't fair?" asked Molly.

"It isn't fair for the big boys to have all the fun," said Edward. "I want to go to that cabin," he added with a frown, "and I can go all by myself, if I want to."

Molly was not paying much attention to Edward, for John was trying to climb up on the porch railing. He was very strong and lively for a baby his age and never so happy as when he was climbing. Molly caught him in her arms. "You're a little monkey," she told him.

"Someday we are going to find you climbing up a tree!"

"Tree," said John.

Molly hugged him. "Let's go to the back yard and see the apple tree," she said.

When lunch time came, Alicia rang the dinner bell and Molly brought John into the house. The twins were already in their chairs, but they had been playing outdoors and their faces and hands were dirty. "I helped Mrs. Meek cook our lunch," Alicia was saying, when she suddenly noticed the twins' faces. "Go and wash your faces," she said. "Ask Edward to help you."

"Edward!" called Molly.

Edward did not answer. And when Molly called a second time he still did not come. Since Edward was Molly's responsibility, she had to let her lunch cool on her plate while she went to look for him. He was not on the front porch or anywhere in the yard. Molly went upstairs, but he was not in his room. He was not on the widow's walk, either.

"I can't find Edward," said Molly, when she returned to the dining room.

"He's a naughty boy, not to come and eat his lunch," said Mrs. Meek.

"He is just absent-minded sometimes," explained Alicia. She and Molly both thought that Edward would come home soon.

But later, when the twins and John were having naps and Alicia had gone over to Becky's house, Molly walked all around the block, looking for Edward. She stopped at Millicent's house, but Millicent had not seen him. Edward was nowhere to be found, and neither was Hugo.

There was nothing strange about Hugo's disappearance, since he was never very far from Edward. Molly knew that wherever Edward had gone, Hugo had followed. What made her suddenly feel anxious, was remembering Edward's disappointment at not being invited to go on the camping trip. Hunter was going on the trip and Edward liked Hunter, who treated him as though he were a big boy too.

She tried to remember just what Edward had said. It was something about the cabin and how he could get there by himself. That is where Edward has gone, thought Molly. But she was sure he had never been to Bear Cabin before.

Molly had never been to Bear Cabin either. But her eyes were bright, and she never missed any signs on the highway. When she had been in the car she had often noticed a sign, shaped liked an arrow, that said *To Bear Cabin.*

But had Edward ever noticed that sign? Molly did not know. Edward was apt to be thinking of something else. He would be quite safe if he could catch up with the other boys, but if they were too far ahead he would probably get lost.

I will have to go after Edward and bring him back, thought Molly. She went through the quiet house and up the stairs. There was no use telling Mrs. Meek where she was going, for Mrs. Meek did not understand Edward. She must tell Alicia, though, so that Alicia would not worry if it took her a long time to get back home.

Alicia was still at Becky's house, so Molly wrote a note which Alicia would be sure to see. *I have gone after Edward,* she wrote, in very large letters. She pinned the note to Alicia's pillow and tiptoed downstairs. Mrs. Meek did not hear her go, and the twins did not wake up.

It was early in the afternoon when Molly left home, and Edward had been missing for at least two hours. Molly looked to left and right as she hurried along the street, for she thought that Edward might have stopped to play with a friend instead of trying to follow his brothers. Edward liked to dawdle. But once he made up his mind, Edward could be very determined.

10

THE TRAIL TO BEAR CABIN

About an hour after Molly had gone to look for Edward, Alicia came back from Becky's house to take care of John. He and the twins were still asleep and Mrs. Meek was resting, so Alicia went to the pink room to get her favorite book. There she saw the note that Molly had pinned to her pillow, telling her that she had gone after Edward. The note did not surprise Alicia. Edward was Molly's charge, and she thought it was quite right for her to go and look for him.

Meanwhile, Molly had come to the sign that said *To Bear Cabin*. It was farther along the highway than she had remembered, because when she had passed it before she had been in a car, and this time she was traveling on her own two feet. The arrow-shaped sign pointed down an unpaved road that led past a farmhouse and a big red barn. Molly gazed far down the highway before she followed the pointing sign. There was no boy in sight, and there was no dog. Edward must have read the sign and turned here, thought Molly. She decided to ask at the farmhouse if anyone had seen him.

The farmer and his wife were used to seeing campers hiking past their home on the way to Bear Cabin. But they were surprised to see a little girl all by herself, and they looked at Molly curiously as she came up the path. The farmer's wife, who was watering a rosebush, smiled. "Aren't you one of the Hubbard children?" she asked.

"Yes, I am Molly, the middle one," said Molly.

"I am Mrs. Hall," said the farmer's wife.

"I know you," said Molly. Mrs. Hall brought fresh eggs to Mother once a week. "Have you seen my little brother Edward?"

"I don't know their names," said Mrs. Hall. "But some of your brothers passed by here this morning."

"Tom and Rufus and Reginald," said Molly. Then she asked, "How far is Bear Cabin from here?"

"A long way," said Mr. Hall, speaking for the first time.

"Not too far," said Mrs. Hall. "It is just up Hunters Hill."

After a drink of cold water, Molly turned to go. But Mrs. Hall said, "Wait. Are you going to the cabin?" Molly nodded. "There's a trail that goes up through the woods," Mrs. Hall went on. "You can't miss it; the trees are marked with red and white stripes."

Molly was eager to see the trees with the red

and white stripes, and she hurried along the road, which sloped upward through the woods. She did not know that Mrs. Hall was watching her anxiously, and she could not hear what she was saying to Mr. Hall.

Up and up the road curved. This is Hunters Hill, thought Molly. Pines, birches, and dark green cedars were on both sides of her. Then all at once she saw a tree that was different from the others, because it was marked with a bright red stripe and a gleaming white one.

Molly paused. Farther ahead was another tree with stripes. This was the trail that led to Bear Cabin. She was starting on toward the farther tree when she heard a sound behind her. It was the rattling, bumpy sound of a very old car. The sound surprised Molly, for she did not see how anyone could drive a car—especially an old one—up that winding trail. She stepped to one side and waited for the car to pass her. It did not pass her, though. Mr. Hall was driving it, and he opened the door and said to Molly, "Hop in."

"Can you drive to Bear Cabin?" asked Molly.

"Part way," said Mr. Hall. "This old car is better than a new one for roads like this."

It's not a road; it's a trail, thought Molly. But she got inside the car. Old as it was, it could travel faster than she could, and she was tired, and very anxious to get to Bear Cabin. She knew she would find her older brothers with Hunter and his father, and she hoped she would discover that Edward was there too. For Edward was not in the town, and he was not on the highway; and if he was not with the campers, where could he be?

Hunter's father was showing the boys how to build a real campfire. It was only five o'clock, but they were all hungry. One boy was getting hot dogs ready; another was fetching plates. They could eat in the cabin or on the porch, but they preferred to gather around a real campfire, since they were campers.

"It's fun not having any girls around," said Rufus.

Just at that moment, a girl appeared! It was Molly, and Mr. Hall was with her. They had left the car on the trail below and climbed the rest of the way.

"Molly!" cried Reginald. "What are you doing here?"

"Has anything happened at home?" asked Tom, stepping forward.

"I brought your little sister part way in my car. She was set on finding you," said Mr. Hall.

While they were speaking, Molly was looking all around for Edward. He was not there. "Oh, Tom, where is Edward?" she said.

"Edward? Edward didn't come with us," said Tom. "What's the matter, Molly? Is Edward lost?"

Molly was so tired that she couldn't help crying as she told the campers about her search for Edward. "I thought he must be here," she said. "He wasn't anywhere else. And he said something about how he could get to the cabin."

Until Molly said *cabin,* none of the boys had

felt especially worried about Edward. Edward often wandered away by himself, but he always showed up again, sooner or later. But if Edward had gone to a cabin! Rufus spoke first, though both Tom and Reginald had the same thought. "Edward must have meant the island cabin," said Rufus. "That's the only one he's been to, and he knows how to paddle."

Never once had Molly thought of the island cabin. Edward was too small to manage a canoe. But when Reginald said, "That is just what Edward would try to do," Molly felt sure that he was right.

There was no supper cooked at Bear Cabin that evening. The campfire was put out and the cabin door was locked. Hunter's father and Mr. Hall both said how dangerous it would be if a little boy Edward's age went out alone in a canoe. It was Hunter who reminded them that even if Edward had been able to find a key to the boathouse, he could not possibly carry out a canoe by himself.

"People are sometimes careless, though," his

father replied. "I have seen a canoe left outside the boathouse more than once."

It was lucky that Mr. Hall had come with Molly to Bear Cabin and that his car was parked down the trail, for that meant a rescue party could start out right away. A lot of people were going to look for Edward this time. Molly put her hand in Tom's and went down toward the car. Mr. Hall said he would drive everyone straight to the river, but Tom told Molly that just as soon as they reached the town he would ask Mr. Hall to stop at their house and leave her there.

"Only men should be in a rescue party," said Tom. He was the oldest of nine children and he spoke firmly.

"Perhaps Edward will be at home," said Molly in a small voice. She could not bear to think of Edward alone on the river. It was almost dark as they drove down the trail, but the car had bright headlights, and Molly watched them flash on the red-and-white-striped trees.

11

WHAT HAPPENED TO EDWARD

While the rescue party was driving down the trail from Bear Cabin, Mrs. Meek was cooking supper at the Hubbard house. There were only four Hubbard children there, and Mrs. Meek was worried because Molly and Edward had not come home. "They ought to be home by six o'clock," she said to Alicia.

"Yes, they ought to be," said Alicia. She was worried too. Molly had gone to look for Edward a long time ago, and though Edward was often absent-minded, Molly never was. None of the neighbors had seen Molly or Edward, and Alicia could not imagine where they were. She never thought of Bear Cabin or the island cabin. If she had, she would have felt even more worried.

The twins were not worried a bit. They were much too young. They were on the back porch, taking turns ringing the dinner bell. "You have rung that bell long enough," Mrs. Meek told them. "Come on in the house now, Gordon and Gregory."

"We are ringing the bell for Molly and Edward," said Gregory cheerfully.

"And Hugo," said Gordon. "Here comes Hugo!"

"Hugo!" cried Alicia, and rushed out on the porch. She expected to see Edward and Molly in a minute, but Hugo had come home all alone.

"Good dog, Hugo," said Alicia. "Where are Molly and Edward?" To her surprise, Hugo was dripping wet. "Where have you been?" said Alicia. But Hugo could not tell her. All he could do was bark and wag his tail.

The next surprise for Alicia was Mr. Hall's car, which rattled up to the house just as she was patting Hugo. She ran out to the sidewalk to see who had come, and Molly jumped out of the car and ran to meet her. "Oh, Alicia, has Edward come home?" cried Molly.

"No, only Hugo," said Alicia. She was puzzled, for she had expected Molly and Edward to come home together. Instead, Molly had returned in a strange car. All the campers from Bear Cabin seemed to be in the car: Tom and Rufus and Reginald, and Hunter and his father.

"Did you say Hugo came home, Alicia?" asked Tom.

"Yes. And he is as wet as if he had been in the river."

Mr. Hall started the car, and the men and boys drove off, leaving Alicia and Molly alone. Alicia burst into tears. "What has happened to Edward?" she cried.

It was Molly's turn to explain, which she did as well as she could. She told Alicia how she had gone to Bear Cabin and how Edward was not there, and what the big boys had said. "They think that Edward must have gone to that cabin on the island, the one we went to with Father," said Molly.

"Oh!" cried Alicia. "That must be how Hugo got wet. He went with Edward and they both must have fallen in the river." She was so frightened at that thought that tears rolled down her cheeks.

Molly, who had got over her first fright, tried her best to console her. "Perhaps not, Alicia," she said. "Edward can paddle and perhaps he got safely to that nice, cosy cabin."

While the two girls were talking, Mrs. Meek came up behind them. "Well, Molly, I am glad you have come home," she said. "I heard that old car of Mr. Hall's and I am as certain as can be that he and the boys are going to find Edward."

"But what if he fell in the river?" asked Alicia.

"Nonsense," said Mrs. Meek. "A boy like

Edward knows enough not to go near the river."

"There aren't any other boys just like Edward," said Molly.

Mrs. Meek was wrong, and Edward's brothers were right; Edward had gone to the river with only Hugo for company. And as Hunter's father had suggested, he had found a canoe that some careless person had left outside the boathouse. There were two paddles in the canoe, but Edward needed only one. He was quite confident that he could get to the island. He took one paddle out and laid it on the bank. Then he shoved and pushed, and pushed and shoved, until finally he managed to launch the canoe.

"Jump in, Hugo," said Edward. But Hugo would not jump in. He loved his master, but he was wary of the canoe. When Edward pushed off from the shore, his dog barked and whined, but no one else was near the boathouse that Saturday afternoon. Nobody heard Hugo, and nobody saw Edward as he paddled determinedly down the river. The canoe, with only Edward in it, was light as a feather and, like a feather, it whirled and drifted on the swift current.

Edward had paddled once before, but he had never steered, and he could not make the canoe go forward in a straight line. The current carried it down the river, turning this way and that, and Hugo plunged into the water and swam after it. But long before the canoe had drifted around the first bend, Hugo gave up following it and swam back to the shore. He did not go home right away. He stayed on the bank and waited. But when Edward did not come back, he jumped into the water again and made one more vain effort to find him. That was why Hugo was dripping wet when he ran back home at suppertime.

Edward did not come back, and he did not get to the cabin. What happened next, he told his rescuers when they found him. They had seen the paddle on the bank and they knew that their guess was right, so they took two canoes out of the boathouse and sped off down the river.

It was dark on the river by that time and the first small island, which Father had called a dot, showed only as a shadow on the water. Nobody in the rescue party could see the green canoe at all, but Reginald saw a white speck against the shadow. When the white speck moved, he said to the others, "There is Edward!"

"Edward!" shouted Tom and Rufus together.

A faint reply answered them. "Island ahoy!"

It was Edward. He had been stranded for a long, long time. He was chilly in his cotton clothes and he was very hungry, but he did not seem to be the least bit frightened. "I thought somebody would come and find me," he told his brothers.

Edward's canoe had grounded against a tiny island, and he had been too tired, by that time, to try to launch it again. The only thing, ap-

parently, that had troubled him was that he could not get to the island with a cabin. He had thought the others were all there, and he wanted to surprise them.

"Don't you ever try to surprise us again," said Tom.

The twins and John were fast asleep, but Alicia and Molly and Mrs. Meek were waiting on the front porch when Edward was brought home. They all gathered around him, making sure that he was safe and sound, and they did not even hear Mr. Hall drive away.

Edward had done a dangerous thing. But he was home again, and no one felt like scolding him just yet. The two girls listened wide-eyed to the story of his adventure, told partly by Edward and partly by his brothers.

"Oh, Edward," said Molly. "Weren't you scared?"

"No," replied Edward. "I'm hungry, though."

"But you might have been drowned," said Mrs. Meek.

Edward looked surprised. He had never once thought of drowning.

"There is just one thing to do," said Tom, after Edward was fed and put to bed. "From now on, we boys will have to look after Edward."

Rufus agreed. "We'll take him with us when we go anywhere."

"Yes. That would be safer," said Reginald.

When the telephone rang a little while later, Molly answered it. "Hello. Is that Molly?" said Mother's voice. "Is everything all right?"

"Yes," said Molly. How glad she was that Mother had not called up earlier!

12

THE APPLE TREE

Father and Mother came back from the mountains the next afternoon, and they were happy to see all their nine children again. "What did you do while we were away?" asked Mother.

"I looked for Edward," Molly began.

"I looked for the boys," interrupted Edward.

"We rescued Edward when Molly couldn't find him," said Tom.

"Begin at the beginning, please, children," said Mother. So little by little Father and Mother heard the whole story. When they learned how Molly had searched for Edward and learned where Edward was found, they agreed with the three big boys that they should look after Edward.

Edward should not have gone to the river all by himself. He was very naughty, even though he had not meant to be. As for Molly, she had tried to take care of him; but he was a boy, and he wanted to do what the other boys did.

"Edward is a little boy with big ideas," said Father.

"Big ideas are dangerous when you are little," said Mother.

Molly looked at Edward, feeling rather sad that he was no longer going to be her responsibility. You never could tell what he would do, and he caused a lot of trouble, but she would miss him when he went off with the three big boys.

Molly sighed. Then suddenly she remembered her diary, which she had meant to write in every single day. A lot of things had been happening for her to write about, but she had been too busy to think about her diary. She went to find it, and when she had found it she wandered out to the apple tree and climbed up the ladder to her own secret perch. She felt as carefree as a bird, for Father and Mother were home again, and Tom was showing Edward how to ride his bicycle.

Boys liked to do boys' things, thought Molly, and girls liked to do girls' things. She looked forward to playing with her best friends, Carol and Sarah. Carol was coming back from camp in just a few more days, and Sarah would soon be back from the mountains. Molly fished in her apron pocket. Where was her diary? She was sure that she had carried it out to the apple tree. If she was going to write in it she had better hurry, before somebody interrupted her.

"Molly!"

That was one of the twins.

"Molly!" There was the other.

"I found a little book," said Gordon, gazing up into the tree.

"Is it your little book?" asked Gregory. "I made a picture in it."

"Twins!" cried Molly, climbing hastily down the ladder.

She seized her diary. But its pages were scribbled over with red and blue and green crayon marks. She wanted to be cross with the twins, but she could not be cross when they earnestly begged her to draw a picture for them.

After all, she had dropped the little book herself—and writing things down in it was a lot of trouble. It was hard finding peace and quiet when you lived in a large family, and Molly was not sure that she wanted peace and quiet. She settled herself on the grass to draw pictures for the twins, when suddenly she heard a cry. "Look at me!"

There was John, standing on the top rung of the ladder. "Look at me," he repeated, very proud of himself.

Molly ran to catch him before he fell off the ladder. John was going to be a lot like Edward, she thought.